Two Monsters

David McKee

Bradbury Press · New York

Library of Congress Cataloging-in-Publication Data   McKee, David. Two monsters. Summary: Two monsters
living on opposite sides of a mountain, who can't agree on whether day is arriving or night departing, insult each
other and hurl rocks until the mountain is destroyed and they make a startling discovery. [1. Monsters — Fiction]
I. Title.   PZ7.M19448Twc   1986   [E]   85-22344   ISBN 0-02-765760-4   10 9 8 7 6 5 4 3 2 1

There was once a monster that lived on the west side of a mountain.

On the east side of the mountain lived another monster.

Sometimes the monsters spoke to each other through a hole in the mountain.

But they never saw each other.

One evening the first monster called through the hole, "Can you see how beautiful it is? Day is departing."

"Day departing?" the second monster called back. "You mean night arriving, you twit!"

"Don't call me a twit, you dumbo, or I'll get angry." He was so annoyed that he could not sleep.

The second monster was also annoyed, and did not sleep either.

The next morning the first monster felt awful after such a bad night. "Wake up, you numbskull," he shouted. "Night is leaving."

"Don't be stupid, you peabrain!" shouted the second monster. "That is day arriving." And he picked up a stone and threw it over the mountain.

"Rotten shot! You missed! You fat ignoramus!" He picked up a bigger stone and hurled it back.

"You hairy, long-nosed nincompoop!" shouted the second monster. He threw a rock and knocked off the top of the mountain.

"You're a stupid old wind-filled prune!" shouted the first monster and he threw a boulder that knocked another chunk off the mountain.

"And you are a bow-legged, soggy cornflake!"

As the day passed, the insults grew longer and longer and the rocks grew bigger and bigger.

The first monster threw yet another giant boulder. "You're a hairy, overstuffed, empty-headed mess!"

"You're a pathetic, addlebrained, smelly, lily-livered custard tart!" screamed the second monster, hurling an even bigger boulder that smashed the last of the mountain.

For the very first time the monsters saw each other.

"Incredible," said the first monster. "Night is arriving. You were right."

"Amazing," said the second monster. "You were right. Day is leaving."

They decided to watch the sunset together.